PARTY NIGHTMARE
WATER WATCHDOG

FANTAIL PUBLISHING,
AN IMPRINT OF PUFFIN ENTERPRISES

Published by the Penguin Group
27 Wrights Lane, London W8 5TZ England

Viking Penguin Inc., 375 Hudson Street, New York, New York
10014, USA.
Penguin Books Australia Ltd. Ringwood, Victoria, Australia.
Penguin Books Canada Ltd., 2801 John Street, Markham,
Ontario, Canada LR3 1BA.
Penguin Books (NZ) Ltd., 182-190 Wairau Road Auckland 10
New Zealand.
Penguin Books Ltd., Registered Offices: Harmondsworth,
Middlesex, England.

First Published by The Berkley Publishing Group 1990
First Published in the UK by Penguin Books 1990

10 9 8 7 6 5 4 3 2 1

0140 903127

PARTY NIGHTMARE

A Novel by Nancy E. Krulik
Based on the Al Burton Production LASSIE
Adapted from the episode "TRAPPED"
Written by Bob Hamner

CHAPTER
1

The bright white tennis ball flew out of Will McCulloch's slingshot and soared gracefully through the air. Lassie watched it as it moved. As soon as she could pinpoint the ball's direction of flight, the golden brown and white purebred collie bent her back legs slightly, gave a little leap, and took off after it. She moved gracefully along the rich green grass of the Mc-Culloch family's front lawn. She ran quickly, anxious to get in front of the ball before it fell. In a split second she had achieved her goal and was standing still, waiting for the ball to drop to a level where she could reach it. As soon as it did, the playful collie turned, opened her wide jaws, and leaped up in the air, catching the ball in mid-flight.

Ten-year-old Will McCulloch and his best

1

friend, Arnie Fielding, watched the scene with amazement.

"Fantastic!" Arnie shouted in amazement.

"I told you Lassie could do it," Will said proudly.

"I didn't mean Lassie," Arnie giggled. "I meant the slingshot."

Will looked at Arnie and shrugged. Obviously Arnie didn't appreciate a talented dog when he saw one. Will turned his attention to his beautiful collie.

"Here, Lassie," he called as he clapped his hands to encourage her. "Bring!"

The beautiful brown and white purebred's tail wagged excitedly as she proudly strolled back to her master with her prize. When she reached Will, Lassie dropped the ball at his feet, and looked up at him with her brown, soulful eyes, awaiting his praise for a job well done.

She was not disappointed. "Good girl," Will said as he lovingly patted her broad brown and white back. Then Will turned to look as a third boy from his fourth grade class rode up the driveway on a shiny black and yellow state-of-the-art BMX bicycle.

"Hi, Latimer," Will called to the boy. Arnie said nothing. Arnie didn't like Jonathan Latimer one bit. He thought Jonathan was one mean bully.

Will, on the other hand, didn't dislike Jonathan. Will was new to Glen Ridge. His family had only recently moved to the small suburban town from San Diego, so Will didn't really know anyone well enough to pass judgment on him.

"You're coming to my party, aren't you, Will?" Jonathan asked as he strolled jauntily onto the lawn.

"I didn't know I was invited," Will answered honestly.

"Sure you are," Jonathan said from behind a cocky grin. "It's for all my friends in the class—at my grandfather's plant nursery. It's an annual event!"

The party sounded great to Will. "I'd like to come," he said brightly.

Lassie watched Will and this new boy very carefully. The collie had never seen Jonathan Latimer before, but there was something about the tall, dark-haired boy that Lassie just didn't like. "Grrr," she growled softly from her place by Will's side.

"Sorry, no pets allowed," Jonathan said to both Will and Lassie.

Will petted Lassie gently on her noble head,

but nodded at Jonathan. "What about Arnie?" Will asked. Arnie was standing far from the other boys, silently watching Will, his best friend, talk to Jonathan, his arch enemy.

"He's not my friend," Jonathan declared loudly enough for Arnie to hear him. Arnie said nothing, but his freckled face grew as red as his hair.

"He's a friend of mine!" Will declared loyally.

Jonathan looked from Arnie to Will. "Okay, bring him," he said finally. Then he walked back to his bike and rode off.

When he was sure Jonathan was gone for good, Arnie finally spoke. "You're not going, are you?" he asked hesitantly.

"We both are," Will responded.

"Thanks a lot," Arnie moaned sarcastically.

"What's that supposed to mean?"

Arnie walked over to Will and looked him straight in the eye. "You don't know him. His family just about started this town!"

"Arnie, I'm not stupid. I live on Latimer Road! It's named for his great-grandfather!" Will exclaimed with a slightly exasperated sigh.

Arnie took a deep breath. It wasn't going to be easy to describe Jonathan to Will. "Maybe

Jonathan is popular," he began, "but he's the biggest practical joker in school. He's got this List of Jerks he puts on the bulletin board in school. Everybody knows it's him, but nobody says anything. It's really embarrassing."

Will looked at his friend with new understanding. "Did you ever make the list?" he asked Arnie quietly.

Arnie's face grew an even brighter red. His whole being was filled with anger and embarrassment. "Yeah, once . . . right at the top!" Arnie admitted. Then he looked at Will with a serious stare. "You'd better watch out for him, Will!"

Will thought about that for a moment. Then he turned and picked up the slingshot, loaded up the ball, pulled back the rubber band, and shot another high fly for Lassie to catch.

Meanwhile, inside the McCullochs's house, Will's parents were chatting in the living room.

"If I can restore the fireplace, I could have the inside track on the whole Stonehaven Mansion," Chris McCulloch said enthusiastically to his wife, Dee. The Stonehaven Mansion was owned by the Latimers, who besides being Jonathan's parents, were also the most powerful family in Glen Ridge. If Chris could get the fireplace contract, it could mean a lot of new business for his construction company. The McCullochs had moved to suburban Glen Ridge from San Diego so Chris could start his own business, and Chris knew that one big contract could do wonders for a new company.

Dee looked up from the mail she was sorting on her desk in the family room. "Did you say Stonehaven?" she asked.

"Is there another sixty-acre estate in Glen Ridge?" he teased.

Dee grinned. "Chris, you may get work there, but I've been invited to a party there!" she announced excitedly, waving a creamy white, engraved invitation in the air.

"Sounds great," Chris said in a less than enthusiastic voice.

Dee began to read excitedly from the invitation. "Cocktails and dinner . . . black-tie . . . It's a charity ball . . . We've got to go, Chris!"

Chris wasn't as thrilled by the invitation as his wife was. "I don't know," he said. "Black-tie. I hate black-tie."

Dee wasn't really listening. She was already thinking of the party. "I'll need a new dress . . ." she thought out loud.

"How much are the tickets?" Chris asked, waking Dee from her daydream.

"Two hundred fifty dollars," Dee said quickly.

Chris clasped his hands together. "Apiece! I'll barely break even on the fireplace!"

"Two hundred fifty a couple," Dee corrected him. "C'mon, Chris, let's go . . . It'll be fun!"

"That depends on your idea of fun." Chris sighed as he played absentmindedly with his bushy moustache.

Just then, Will came bounding into the house, a happy Lassie following close at his heels.

"Wait 'til you hear," he announced to his parents. "I got invited to a party . . ."

"Don't tell me—it's at Stonehaven Mansion," Chris interrupted glumly.

Will looked at his father in confusion. He had no idea what Chris was talking about. "No, the party's at Latimer's Nursery."

Chris shrugged and got up to leave.

"Chris . . ." Dee started.

"Look, let's talk about it later," Chris said over his shoulder as he went up the stairs to his office.

Will watched his father leave. "Lassie and

I just came in for a healthy snack," he said to his mother in an attempt to change the subject.

"Right," Dee laughed. "You can't eat supper on an empty stomach."

CHAPTER
2

The next morning Jonathan Latimer woke up extra early. He was anxious to begin setting up for his party. Jonathan got dressed in record time, gulped down his breakfast, and ran outside to get his bike. Then he pedaled as quickly as he could down the road and over to the wooded acreage his family called Latimer's Nursery. The nursery was known all over Northern California for its fine, healthy plant life.

As soon as he reached the nursery's main greenhouse, Jonathan hopped off his bike and ran into the building to get some heavy rope.

Jonathan had planned a special game for this party. He was constructing a maze. Jonathan's guests would have to use their hands to follow the path of the rope while they were

blindfolded! Jonathan grinned as he started lay-
ing out the path. He knew the maze would lead
to a surprise—a surprise that everyone would
find hysterical, except for Will McCulloch!

"That sucker won't like this one bit," Jonathan chuckled out loud, "but I will!"

Quickly Jonathan knotted the rope around
trees and over hills. He dragged it through the
front door of an old tool shed and out the back
door. Jonathan was so busy setting up his nasty
game that he didn't even notice the creaking of
the old rotting floorboards that lay beneath him
as he tied the rope to a post in the old supply
shed.

Back at the McCullochs's house everyone's
thoughts were on parties. At the breakfast table,
Dee was trying to adjust to the idea that she
might not be able to convince Chris to go to the
charity ball after all.

"I can think of one hundred reasons to go,
but I know there are two hundred and fifty reasons why we can't," Dee said, referring to the
cost of the tickets.

"It's not that we can't afford it," Chris explained. "It's just that . . ."

"I know, you hate crowds," Dee finished her husband's thought.

"Look," Chris said. "If I were going to do it, you're one of a handful of women I would do it for."

Dee scowled and gave Chris a playful shove. "Thanks, you're a real sport," she said, laughing.

"What's so funny?" fourteen-year-old Megan McCulloch asked her parents as she wandered into the kitchen in her robe and slippers.

"Good morning, Sleepyhead. Happy Saturday." Dee smiled at her daughter as she used her hands to muss up Megan's already disheveled blonde mane. "I'd love to stay and chat, but I've got to run a few errands. See you later."

Megan poured herself a bowl of cereal, and brought it over to the table. She carried the box with her, too. Megan always read the cereal box with breakfast. It was an old habit.

"I'm excited about you guys going to that party at Stonehaven," she said to her father from behind her box.

"We're not exactly going. To tell the truth, I don't like big parties!"

Megan glanced up from the nutritional information on the box and looked understandingly at her dad. "I know what you mean. All those strange people, and worrying about whether or not you're saying the right thing . . ."

"Something like that," Chris responded softly. Then he got up and walked out of the kitchen.

Megan watched him for a second, then she shrugged and went back to her reading.

Upstairs, Will was getting ready for Jonathan's party. As he dressed, Arnie's warnings rang through his head. But Will dismissed all his bad thoughts. Arnie had to be wrong about Jonathan, Will convinced himself. After all, Jonathan had ridden over to personally invite him to the party, hadn't he? Arnie just wasn't giving Jonathan a chance, Will decided.

Will checked himself in the mirror one last time. Then he went outside and hopped on his bike.

Lassie was taking her late morning nap under the shade of her favorite tree when she heard the screen door slam. As she groggily opened one eye, she saw Will mount his bike. Immediately she stood and shook the sleep from her body.

"Ruff! Ruff!" Lassie barked. It was as

though she were calling to Will, "Hey! Wait for me!"

Will looked over his shoulder, smiled, and motioned for Lassie to hurry up.

Lassie pulled her mouth back in a joyous collie smile and ran to catch up with Will. As soon as she was by his side, Will started pedaling. Together the boy and his ever-faithful dog traveled to the party.

After a few minutes Will turned onto the narrow dirt road that led to Latimer's Nursery. As soon as they reached the main gate, Will stopped short and looked down toward Lassie.

"Time for you to go home," he told her.

Lassie hesitated for a moment. She wasn't sure what it was that made her feel the way she did, but the sensitive collie just had the notion that there was danger afoot. She wanted to stick with Will—just in case he needed her for any reason.

But Will couldn't know what his collie was thinking. All he knew was that he wanted to join in the fun and he couldn't until Lassie left.

"Come on, you heard Jonathan. No pets!"

Lassie looked sadly at Will and then turned to leave. She traveled a few feet down the road. But as soon as her sensitive ears picked up the sound of Will pedaling off toward the party, she stopped, moved to the side of the road, and lay down under a tree. She stretched out her long, lean front legs and lay her head down on her forepaws. She would wait for Will after all.

By the time Will reached the greenhouse, the party was in full swing. There were several picnic tables, each one covered with sodas, chips, and candies. Two six-foot-long hero sandwiches stuffed with all kinds of cheeses and cold cuts lay in the center of the tables. There were about a dozen boys and girls at the party. Will recognized almost all of them from his class at school. Most of the kids were laughing and listening to the rock 'n' roll music that was coming from two large speakers that had been set up in the greenhouse. Will spotted Arnie sitting all by himself on a bench under a shady tree. Will walked over to Arnie and sat next to him on the bench.

"Boy, am I glad you're here," Arnie said as Will sat. He nodded over to a tree across the way where Jonathan and his best friend, Wayne, were whispering and giggling. "I think those two are up to something," Arnie told Will.

Will was about to tell Arnie he was being

silly when Jonathan picked up the end of a rope and called to everyone to gather around.

"Okay, listen up," he said. "The name of the game is Danger Trail. The idea is that everybody takes a turn following the trail blindfolded, finds the whistle at the end of the rope, blows the whistle at the end, and waits for the next guy. The one who finishes fastest, wins. And no cheating."

"I don't like this," Arnie whispered to Will.

"Come on, Arnie," Will said.

"Now, all we need is a volunteer to be first . . ." Jonathan continued looking at the crowd. "Look, we have someone—Will McCulloch!"

Arnie jumped up. "Hey! Will didn't volunteer!" he shouted.

Wayne stood up and looked at Arnie threateningly. Wayne was bigger than most of the kids in the class, so he could really look scary when he wanted to.

"You mean he's gonna wimp out?" Wayne asked with a menacing note in his voice.

Will stood up nervously. He didn't particularly want to go first, but he didn't want to be called a wimp either! "Well if no one else wants to go . . ." he began.

"Don't do it," Arnie cautioned Will. "Why don't you go, Wayne?" Arnie challenged.

Wayne looked at Jonathan and smirked. "Okay," he said.

Jonathan handed Wayne the end of the rope and tied the blindfold around his eyes. Then Jonathan took a stopwatch from his pocket. As he clicked down the timer, Jonathan shouted, "Ready. Set. Go!"

Wayne held on to the rope and inched along slowly. The rope had been fastened at regular intervals to fence posts and around tree trunks. Wayne made his way into the woods. When he was absolutely sure no one would see him, Wayne ripped off the blindfold. Then he walked comfortably along the path, which took him over a bridge and through the old shed before he reached the other end of the rope. The last bit of rope was tied around a tree just at the edge of a deep pit filled with mushy, smelly brown mud! If Wayne hadn't taken off the blindfold he surely would have fallen in the pit! Wayne spotted the whistle hanging from the tree and took it in his hand.

Toot! Toot!

The sound of the whistle traveled through the air until it reached the crowd of kids by the greenhouse. Jonathan stopped his stopwatch and marked the time on a small pad. Then he turned to Will and picked up the rope. "Now it's your turn," he said.

Arnie grabbed Will's arm. "You don't have to do this," Arnie urged.

Will shook himself free from Arnie's grasp. "Arnie relax," he said, grabbing the rope from Jonathan.

"This *is* me relaxed," Arnie mumbled to himself as he watched Jonathan blindfold Will.

Jonathan smiled a sly, knowing grin. "Okay, McCulloch," he said. "Ready. Set. Go!"

CHAPTER
3

Will took a deep, quivering breath before he began inching his way along the roped path. This whole game made him very nervous. In a way Will wished he could have taken Arnie's advice and refused to go. But the thought of being called a wimp in front of his whole class was more upsetting to Will than any scary game Jonathan Latimer could come up with. So Will kept on walking, holding tight to the thick, itchy woven rope.

Eventually, the sound and feel of dried leaves crackling under his feet let Will know that he was in the woods, out of sight of his classmates. It would be easy for him to pull off his blindfold now. No one would ever know. But

Will never cheated—no matter how scary the game was.

Over by the greenhouse, Jonathan waited until Will was far into the woods and out of hearing before he turned to face his party guests.

"Okay, come on," Jonathan said, motioning for the others to follow him as he started hiking off in the exact opposite direction than the one Will had just taken.

"Where?" Arnie demanded to know.

"You'll find out," Jonathan said with a smile so sinister it made Arnie shiver.

"I hope Will's okay," Arnie whispered quietly to himself as he followed the others.

Arnie wasn't the only one concerned about Will. As Lassie lay quietly under the tree she felt a nervous feeling gnawing away at her stomach. She couldn't help thinking that this boy Jonathan Latimer did not really consider himself a friend of Will's and that, in fact, he was out to cause her beloved Will harm.

Ordinarily, Lassie was very careful to obey any order from a member of her family. But at this particular moment, Lassie's desire to be obedient was far outweighed by her desire to protect her best friend. At that moment, Lassie decided to ignore Will's order to stay away from the party. She stood and ran swiftly through the entrance and on to the nursery grounds.

"La la la," Will sang quietly to himself as he slowly followed the rope trail hand over hand. Singing kept his mind occupied so he was less afraid. "Just gotta keep calm," he reminded himself. "This will be over soon." Will made his way through the dark forest, past the rows of trees, over the rickety bridge, and along the leaf-covered dirt road until he reached the old supply shed Jonathan had been in earlier.

Creak. Creak. The rotting floorboards in the shed were noisy under Will's sneakers. The quiet of the forest made the frightening creaky noise seem much louder than it really was. Will began to feel like he was in some old haunted house attraction at a county fair. Anxiously, Will sniffed at the air. The shed was musty, and the combination of the smells of mold, rotting leaves, and chemical fertilizer gave the place a very unpleasant stench.

"Where am I?" Will asked out loud to nobody. Very slowly, Will took another gentle, cautious step.

Nancy E. Krulik

CRASH! BOOM! Almost immediately the floorboards cracked in half and fell out from under the boy's feet! Will fell with a rough thud to the ground below! The fall took the blind-folded boy by surprise. His heart began to pound so hard he felt as though it would leap from his heart!

"HELP ME! HELP ME, PLEASE!" he shouted into the darkness. It took Will only a second to remember the blindfold. Quickly he ripped it off and looked around with dazed eyes.

Will had fallen into a dirt-packed area just below the shed floor. At the moment, Will was sitting underneath the shed. He tried to straighten his legs to stand, but the area around him was too close and cramped to allow the boy any movement. He reached up to grab a floor-board to pull himself up on, but he couldn't reach. Frustrated, Will sat still and studied his surroundings. It wasn't a very pleasant place. The nearly-complete darkness was broken only by a narrow stream of sunlight that was making its way through the cracks in the floorboards over Will's head. Piles of loose dirt surrounded Will on all sides. Worst of all, the almost cons-tant creaking of the floorboards served as a con-

22

tinuing reminder to Will that the whole shed could cave in on him at any time.

Will felt sick to his stomach. He wasn't going to be able to get out of this one alone. And if someone didn't come by with help soon, he would be buried alive!

"HELLO! HELLO!" Will cried out desperately. "Can anybody hear me?"

Somebody did hear him. Lassie stopped short on the dirt road. Her triangular ears stood straight up on the sides of her noble head. Lassie's sensitive ears were picking up sounds that Jonathan and the others could never have heard.

"HELLO! HELLO!"

Fear filled Lassie's whole body. Those shouts were Will's! And from the sound of the panic in his voice, he was in serious trouble! Without a thought for herself, Lassie took off in the direction of the shouts. She ran so quickly that she looked like nothing more than a brown and white blur moving in and out of the trees. Lassie took no notice of the pounding of her great heart or the pain in her paws as she ran over sharp rocks. She was a dog with a single thought on her mind—she must save her master.

"GRUFF! GRUFF!"

Lassie's concentration was broken suddenly by the deep, dangerous barks of an angry Doberman tied to a tree. The sleek, black, medium-sized dog was barking wildly and jumping up, trying to attack Lassie. It was the Doberman's job to scare off intruders in the nursery, and he did not like the idea of another dog walking on his land.

"Gruff! Gruff!" The Doberman made another vicious lunge in Lassie's direction. Lassie leaped backwards. The only thing keeping the Doberman from the collie was a metal link safety chain which barely succeeded in keeping the Doberman tied to his post by the tree.

Lassie studied the dog. She stared at his clipped tail and trimmed ears. His body was long and lean and his coat brushed and shiny. The Doberman was obviously well cared for. Lassie took a hard look at her opponent's long legs. It wasn't difficult for Lassie to realize that this wildly angry dog was a fast runner who, should the situation arise, would probably outrun and capture her. The white fur on the collie's chest rose. For the first time in her life, brave Lassie knew fear.

"HELP!!!" Will's screams met Lassie's ears once again. That was all it took to shake the fear from Lassie's heart. The loving collie would gladly give her own life to save the boy she loved. Without another look at the leaping, maniacal Doberman, Lassie ran off to help Will.

As she ran, the brave and loyal collie prayed the chain around the Doberman's neck would hold!

CHAPTER
4

Arnie stared at the slushy, smelly pit of mud in amazement. This trick was too mean, even for Jonathan to play. Arnie could feel his blood boil in anger. "Wait a minute," he called angrily to Jonathan. "You mean Will is supposed to fall into that, blindfolded?"

Jonathan grinned. "Good guess."

"Dumb idea!" Arnie declared, looking to his classmates for support.

Lots of the other kids looked at Jonathan as angrily as Arnie did, but they were all too afraid of making the "List of Jerks" to say anything. Only Wayne was eager to speak.

"I think it's a great idea!" Wayne retorted, patting his buddy Jonathan on the back with a hearty laugh.

Arnie could see nothing funny about such

a mean-spirited joke. Quickly he turned to start down the path. "I'm gonna tell him," he said.

Jonathan grabbed Arnie's shoulder to stop him. Wayne helped out by jumping ahead to block Arnie's path.

"No, you're not!" Jonathan hissed angrily into Arnie's ear.

Arnie moved back in retreat. He was surrounded. One move and Wayne was certain to deck him. There was nothing Arnie could do now but wait. Still, Arnie vowed silently to shout a warning to Will as soon as he saw him head down the trail. Jonathan wouldn't have the chance to stop him then.

It seemed to Arnie that time was passing very slowly. The kids all sat quietly watching the trail. Will was nowhere in sight. Finally Arnie spoke. "Will's been gone a very long time," he announced.

Jonathan looked down at his stopwatch. "Maybe he got lost," Jonathan admitted. "I'll take a look."

"I'll go with you," Arnie said.

"No! You stay right here," Jonathan ordered. Then he turned and headed down the roped trail. Arnie made a move to follow him, but Wayne blocked his way, giving Arnie the dirtiest look the boy had ever seen. Arnie had no choice but to sit and wait with the others.

Jonathan had tried his best not to show it in front of the other kids, especially not Wayne, but the truth was he was worried. Will had been gone almost half an hour—about fifteen minutes longer than the trail should have taken him. As he followed the rope maze in reverse, Jonathan checked the surrounding woods nervously, hoping Will hadn't hurt himself.

Eventually, Jonathan's journey brought him to the old shed. As he entered the shed, Jonathan opened his eyes wide, trying to adjust to the dim light inside. As soon as he looked down, Jonathan gasped. He had spotted the gaping hole in the floor.

The sound of the floor creaking under Jonathan's heavy footsteps was music to Will's frightened ears. "Down here!" Will called anxiously from beneath the floor of the shed.

Jonathan looked at the floor in shock. Will was trapped under there! At that moment, Jonathan knew his little gag had gone too far. Will was in serious trouble! He had to get help! Quickly, Jonathan turned to run out of the shed. But he barely had a chance to move his foot when the creaking floorboards gave way once again. Jonathan landed with a thud—right next to Will.

"AAAAAAH!!!" Jonathan screamed into the darkness.

The boy's screams traveled through the air until they reached the short, clipped ears of the Doberman. Just as Lassie would stop at nothing to save her master, the Doberman would stop at nothing to save Jonathan. Not even a metal chain could keep him away!

Frantically, the Doberman leaped into the air. The chain yanked him right back. With a gruff, frustrated bark, the Doberman lunged again. This time the dog's sensitive ears picked up a "clink" as one of the metal links broke under the strain. Encouraged, the Doberman jumped again, using all his strength to stretch the chain to its limit. Snap! The power of the Doberman's leap finally broke the chain loose from the tree. With a growl of relief, the Doberman took off on its long lean legs into the woods, dragging part of the chain behind him.

Meanwhile, Will was trying his best to keep Jonathan calm as the two boys lay still under the floor of the shed.

"How are we supposed to get out of here?"

Jonathan demanded to know as though this dangerous situation was Will's fault!

"Don't worry, they'll find us," Will said, trying to reassure himself as well as Jonathan.

"Who's worried?" Jonathan countered, trying desperately to keep up his big-shot reputation.

Will didn't say a word. He was very angry with Jonathan for getting him into this mess in the first place. But Will knew that there wasn't any point in arguing with him at this moment. He was going to need Jonathan's help if they were going to get out of this mess alive. So, instead of arguing, the two boys lay side by side in silence, listening to the creaking of the floorboards overhead. Will stayed silent as long as he could. But the noise was getting louder and louder and eventually, Will couldn't take it any more!

Will knew there wasn't time to wait for someone to come with help. The boys would have to escape on their own.

"We've got to do something before this whole thing collapses!" Will told Jonathan with a quivering voice. Then he turned on his side and began to dig into the dirt wall with his bare hands!

Jonathan lay still on the ground, frozen with fear. It had never occurred to him that the old shed might collapse on top of him!

Will gave Jonathan a shove. "Come on!" he ordered. "Maybe we can dig through!"

Jonathan hesitated for just a moment. He wasn't used to taking orders. But soon he was digging side by side with Will.

The boys did not know it, but outside, help was on its way! Lassie had finally made her way to the shed. Using her amazing sense of smell, Lassie had pinpointed Will's location! Now she had come to rescue him.

Happily, Lassie opened her mouth to bark a comforting "I'm here!" call to Will. But before the sound could leave the collie's throat, the Doberman flashed in front of her, blocking her way into the shed. For one, terrifying second, the collie and the Doberman faced each other in a standoff. There was a wild look in the Doberman's eyes. Before the angry Doberman had a chance to jump up and attack her, Lassie's quick reflexes took control of her body. Without so much as a yelp of warning to the other dog, Lassie turned and ran off into the woods!

The Doberman was taken by surprise—but not for long. In seconds he took off and ran at top speed into the woods after Lassie!

CHAPTER
5

Lassie had never run so fast in her whole life. Without ever having to look back to check, the speeding collie was acutely aware that the vicious Doberman was hot on her trail. Lassie didn't have to see him to be aware of his presence. Her keen nose had picked up his scent, and her powerful ears could hear his heavy breathing and quick, approaching footsteps. The Doberman was one fast dog! Lassie knew for certain that she could never outrun him. It was a fact of nature that a Doberman could outrun a collie. Her only chance was to outsmart the Doberman. But Lassie knew the pressure was on. She had to come up with a plan soon, or it would be too late to help Will!

As Lassie raced past the tall elm trees, tiny saplings, full green bushes, and brightly colored flowers that grew throughout the nursery, her brain worked as fast as her legs. She was trying to think of a way to get the Doberman off her trail. As soon as the main greenhouse came into sight, Lassie's big collie mouth pulled back into a great smile. The greenhouse was the answer to her prayers!

Quickly, Lassie steered off the dirt path she had been following through the nursery, and darted over to the greenhouse. The door to the greenhouse had been left partially open. Lassie used her long collie nose to ease the door open the rest of the way, and then snuck silently into the building. The determined dog ignored the heavy beating of her heart. This was no time to be afraid. Lassie knew she needed to keep a clear head for her plan to work. So, as calmly as possible, Lassie slipped behind some large, leafy plants, and waited for the angry Doberman to arrive.

She didn't have to wait very long. The Doberman had followed Lassie's scent into the greenhouse. Lassie watched as the big, dark dog stood at the doorway for just an instant. The Doberman looked around, then followed his nose into the glass building. Lassie moved farther back into the bushes to hide herself from the Doberman's searching eyes.

The Doberman stalked the greenhouse, moving closer and closer to Lassie's hideout. Lassie held her breath as her angry enemy passed by the bushes she was using for protection. Much to her amazement, the big dog walked right past her! Lassie stood silently watching the dog walk to the other side of the greenhouse. When she was sure that she was out of the Doberman's immediate reach, Lassie took a deep breath and leaped out from her spot behind the bushes, heading straight for the greenhouse door!

The sudden movement frightened the Doberman. With a loud bark, he turned and watched as a streak of brown and white fur zoomed across the greenhouse. The Doberman reacted immediately. Without wasting an instant, the dog took a flying leap in Lassie's direction! Luckily, the scheming collie had a big headstart. By the time the Doberman landed, Lassie was already on the other side of the greenhouse doorway. As the Doberman made a move to follow her out the door and into the woods, Lassie used her nose to slam the greenhouse door right in his face!

As soon as she heard the lock catch on the door, Lassie ran back toward the decrepit shed where Will was trapped. She ran with a smile, knowing she was leaving the Doberman barking madly and pawing helplessly at the greenhouse door.

Meanwhile, back at the mud hole, Arnie was getting angry. Jonathan had been gone for at least twenty minutes, and Will had been missing for over an hour. This "game" of Jonathan's had gone on long enough!

"I don't care what Jonathan said," Arnie stood up and announced. "I'm going to look for Will!"

Wayne stood and looked curiously at Arnie. Arnie could feel his body grow tense. But much to Arnie's surprise, Wayne didn't swing at him. Obviously, Wayne was pretty worried, too.

"I don't know . . ." Wayne started.

"Well, I do!" Arnie declared as he turned and started off following the rope maze in reverse.

Seeing that Wayne wasn't going to start any fights, the other kids stood and, one by one, followed Arnie along the path. Wayne watched them leave. He wanted to listen to Jonathan and stay put, but this game was getting pretty creepy. Underneath all of his bully acts, Wayne was pretty much of a scaredy-cat. He didn't want to be left alone in the woods. So, although he hesitated for a minute, Wayne eventually turned and followed close behind the others.

Of course, Will and Jonathan had no idea that help was on its way. The two boys kept digging. And since there was little else for them to do, they talked to one another. It was the first real conversation the two boys had ever had.

"Listen," Jonathan began slowly. "I didn't mean for this to happen . . . It was just supposed to be a joke . . ."

"You mean, like the 'List of Jerks,'" Will interrupted him.

Jonathan looked over at Will with surprise. "How did you know that was me?"

Will snickered. "You're not the only one with friends in the class." He smiled knowingly.

Jonathan was so embarrassed, he turned away from Will and stared at the seemingly endless pile of dirt with despair. "It's no use," he cried. "We'll never get out of here!"

Will looked over to see Jonathan wiping

tears from his eyes. But before he could react, Will heard a familiar voice.

"RUFF! RUFF!"

"Lassie!" Will exclaimed. "It's Lassie!"

Lassie stared down into the hole between the floorboards.

"Wow, am I glad to see you!" Will said gratefully. "Go Lassie! Get help, girl!"

Lassie understood. This was one order from Will she had no problem obeying. In an instant she ran off, racing through the woods in search of the other kids.

As the dog ran across the floor and out the door, the floorboards shifted, and a fresh pile of dirt caved in around the boys.

"HELLLP!" Jonathan screamed hysterically, grabbing on to Will in fear.

"It will be all right. Lassie will get help," Will said slowly, not sure whether he was trying to convince Jonathan or himself.

"RUFF! RUFF!" Lassie barked as loudly as she could, hoping someone would hear her plea for help. "RUFF! RUFF!"

As Arnie and the other kids moved closer to the shed, they heard her cries.

"Hey! That's Lassie, Will's dog!" Arnie announced to the others. "Lassie! Lassie! Over here!" he called.

Lassie breathed a heavy sigh of relief. She had recognized Arnie's friendly voice immediately! Swiftly, Lassie cut across a field of bushes to reach Arnie. She stood by his side for a second. Then she turned her head and pointed her nose in the direction of the shed. Finally she ran a few feet in that direction. Will would have known Lassie well enough to recognize that this was her signal to follow her. But Arnie was confused. He stood still and watched her go.

Lassie was getting frustrated. She had to find a way to get the boy to follow her. Quickly, Lassie raced back to Arnie's side, ran a few feet up the road, stopped, and motioned with her head for Arnie to follow her. To Lassie's great relief, the boy understood this time. Quickly, Arnie ran to Lassie's side and followed the collie down the path to the shed, leaving Wayne and the others trailing just behind.

When they reached the door of the old shed, Lassie stopped short and motioned with her head for Arnie to go in. Gingerly, Arnie walked through the door.

"Will?" he called out nervously.

"Arnie!" Will answered from his spot beneath the floorboards. "Down here, Arnie. Be careful!"

Arnie looked at the hole in the floor and stepped away quickly.

"I don't know how to get you out of there!" Arnie called out desperately.

Before Will had a chance to respond, Lassie took over.

"Ruff! Ruff!" she barked as a command. Obediently, Arnie followed her outside.

"Hurry!" Jonathan called after him.

Outside, Lassie had found an old wooden ladder. It was lying along the side of the shed, hidden behind some potted plants. Eagerly, Arnie and Wayne picked up the ladder and carried it into the shed. Taking great care to watch where they walked, the two boys stood on either side of the hole and slowly lowered the ladder down to Will and Jonathan.

As he watched the ladder descend, Jonathan wiped his eyes and looked earnestly at Will. "You won't say anything will you? he begged desperately. "I mean about . . ." Before Jonathan could say another word, the ladder was in place. Jonathan took hold of the ladder and climbed out of the hole. Will followed close behind.

As soon as Will was out of the hole, Lassie ran over and jumped up to greet him. She licked his face with boundless love and relief.

"It's good to see you too, girl," Will giggled. But the reunion was cut short by the sound of creaking floorboards.

"Let's get out of here!" Will screamed. The four boys and the collie ran out the door as fast as they could!

As soon as they saw Will and Jonathan, the other kids at the party exploded into a loud cheer.

"What happened in there anyway?" Arnie asked Will once the applause had died down.

Jonathan looked anxiously at Will. He hoped Will wouldn't tell everyone that he had been crying.

"Well, I fell in when the floorboards gave way . . . and Jonathan was trying to help me," Will explained tactfully.

Jonathan gave a small sigh of relief. He moved closer to Will and held out his hand in a sign of friendship. "No more 'List of Jerks'," Jonathan promised in a whisper only Will could hear.

"Okay," Will answered quietly.

Jonathan was about to say something else,

but he was drowned out by a loud bang! Jonathan gasped when he realized what had happened. The fragile floorboards had finally given way! Will watched in horror as half of the shed came crashing down to the ground! They had gotten out just in time! Without another word, Will turned and walked away. He had seen enough. Jonathan watched Will go, and then followed him.

After a while, with a look of embarrassment on his face, Jonathan began to tell Will the truth about the "Danger Trail" game. He took Will over to see the mud pile trap he had prepared.

"So the reason you invited me to your party is so I'd wind up neck deep in mud?" Will asked when Jonathan had finished.

Jonathan looked sheepishly at the ground and kicked at the dirt with his toe. "Now it seems like a pretty dumb idea!"

Will grinned. "I don't know . . ." He laughed. "It seems pretty funny to me . . ." Will and Jonathan exchanged a knowing look. Then, together, the two boys took a flying leap right into the mud!

At first, Arnie watched them in horror. But

after watching Will and Jonathan splash around for a bit, Arnie decided to join in the fun!

"Ayayayaya!" Arnie yelled in his best Tarzan imitation as he plunged feet first into the mud. Wayne followed Arnie, and before anyone could say "mud fight!" all the kids were splashing playfully in the mud.

Lassie watched the kids from a comfortable spot under a shady tree. She wasn't planning on joining them. Mud wrestling was not her sport. She much preferred a good game of fetch!

EPILOGUE

It was almost dark by the time Will reached his house. He pulled his bicycle into the garage and then went in the side door and directly into the laundry room. Will stripped out of his clothes and put them in the washing machine—before his parents could see his mud-caked clothes. Then Will wrapped himself in a clean towel and ran upstairs to take a shower. While Will was in the shower, Lassie strolled into the living room. She found Megan sitting on the floor, working on putting together a jigsaw puzzle. Megan had been working on the puzzle all afternoon, and already she was halfway finished with the snow-covered barn that was pictured on the box. Lassie lay down on her soft white belly and put her noble head on Megan's lap. Megan smiled and petted the collie on the head. Then she went back to concentrating on her puzzle.

Eventually Will made his way back downstairs to the family room. He sat down next to Megan, looked at the puzzle, and then reached down and handed Megan the piece she had spent the past five minutes looking for. Megan scowled, but she took the piece and placed it in the puzzle.

"How was the party?" she asked.

"Great! There was tons of food, and we played a really cool game, and guess what—I think Jonathan Latimer's an okay guy!" Will said, all in one excited breath.

"That's not what I've heard!"

Will was quiet for a second, fitting another piece into the puzzle. Then he asked his sister seriously, "Megan, how does he know if anybody likes him because they like him, or because of who he is?"

"You mean, because he's a Latimer?"

Will nodded. "Yeah . . . he says it gets rough sometimes."

"I could learn to live with it," Megan said sarcastically.

Will looked at his sister curiously. "Being a Latimer?" he asked.

"No," Megan explained. "Being a rich Mc-Culloch!"

"Ruff! Ruff!" Lassie's happy bark interrupted Megan and Will's conversation. The kids looked up to see what all the excitement was about.

Megan smiled brightly. Her parents were standing in the doorway—dressed for a black-tie party!

"You're going to Stonehaven!" Megan smiled.

"I'm just going to measure the fireplace," Chris teased, dusting off the lapel of his tuxedo.

"You look great!" Will complimented them.

Dee twirled around so the full skirt of her new satin evening gown flew all around her. "Thank you, sir," she said, giving Will a curtsey.

Will's face grew hot with embarrassment. "I, uh, meant both of you," he muttered.

Chris pulled at his bow tie. "It's the black tie," he said to Dee with a grin. Then he turned to leave.

Megan jumped up from the floor. "Don't go!" she shouted at them.

Dee and Chris turned around with surprise. "What?" they asked together in amazement.

"I mean, don't go until I get my camera,"

Megan explained as she darted up the stairs to her room.

Before long, Megan was back with her most prized possession—her 35-millimeter camera.

"Okay, everyone," Megan directed. "Smile!"

Chris put his arm around Dee and smiled. Megan clicked the shutter on her camera.

"Another one for the family album," she said as she put the lens cover back on the camera.

Dee and Chris turned and walked out the door. Lassie jumped up and tried to follow them, but Will grabbed her by the collar and gently tugged her back.

"You're staying here with Megan and me. You've had enough parties for one day," Will teased Lassie with a hug.

Lassie looked up and licked Will's face with her rough pink tongue. Will was right! A nice night at home with her two favorite kids was just the right kind of evening for a party animal like Lassie!

WATER WATCHDOG

A Novel by Nancy E. Krulik
Based on the Al Burton Production LASSIE
Adapted from the episode "LASSIE AT
LAST "
Written by Joel Rogosin

CHAPTER
1

Click. Click. Click. The sound of the opening and closing of the camera shutter was music to Megan McCulloch's ears. Fourteen-year-old Megan was an avid amateur photographer who had big dreams of someday becoming a famous professional photographer for *Life* magazine. There was nothing Megan liked to do more than spend a peaceful afternoon taking pictures of unusual scenes in out-of-the-way places.

Today Megan had ridden her bike to a small rarely visited wooded area in her hometown of Glen Ridge, California, to take pictures of an old, burned-out, abandoned house that sat by the edge of a lake. Megan had found the house about a week before on one of the long walks she

liked to take in the forests that surrounded Glen
Ridge. Megan loved the feeling of wandering
round the woods alone, with only her beloved
camera for company.

But on this particular afternoon, Megan
was not alone in the forest. She had ridden over
to the lake with her best friend, Lisa. Both girls
were taking a freshman photography class at
Glen Ridge High School, and the pictures they
were shooting were part of a homework assignment for the class. The assignment was to find
an unusual object and photograph it from different angles. Megan figured a burned-out house
was a pretty unusual object. Lisa had long since
finished shooting all thirty-six pictures on her
roll of film, and was having a great time swimming in the lake—wearing nothing more than
her underwear! Megan, on the other hand, took
her photography much more seriously than Lisa
did, and she was still busy taking pictures, carefully checking the burned-out house from all angles and trying to get the most artistic shot of
the remnants of an old chimney.

This shot is sure to earn me an A in photography, Megan thought enthusiastically as she
took a picture of the destroyed chimney surrounded by black ashes and green leafy trees.

Then she placed a bright red wildflower on top of the chimney and took a few more pictures. Megan could almost hear the praise her teacher would give her for that idea: "Such originality!" she would say. Megan took several more shots from that angle before her concentration was broken by a spray of water coming from the lake.

"Hey, cut that out!" Megan shouted sharply to Lisa as she wiped a splash of water from her face.

Lisa giggled. "Put down the camera and come for a swim," Lisa called. Megan looked at her friend sheepishly, and shook her head no.

"What's the big deal, Megan?" Lisa taunted. "It's not like anyone is looking!"

Megan watched as her friend jumped and did a nosedive into the water. Lisa swam underwater for a minute, then popped up, spitting a stream of cool, clear lake water from between her teeth. Megan had to laugh. Lisa looked like the water fountain in the center of Glen Ridge Park.

"Come on, get wet all over," Lisa urged Megan.

Megan hesitated for a minute. Then she

carefully placed her beloved camera back in its black leather case and looked at her watch.

"It's getting kind of late," she muttered uncomfortably, shaking her long mane of blonde hair. "I've got to get home." Megan did not really want to take off her clothes and jump into the water. That wasn't the sort of thing Megan liked to do. It made her slightly nervous. Megan sighed. Lisa would never understand that. Nothing made adventurous, outgoing Lisa nervous.

"You said you would come swimming," Lisa whined. Then, annoyed that Megan had broken her promise, Lisa gave her a dirty look, waved her hand, and paddled a little farther from the shore, leaving Megan all by herself on the bank of the lake.

Reluctantly, Megan stood up and called to Lisa with a wavering voice. "Wait!" she said, looking all around her to make sure the coast was clear. When she was absolutely positive that there was no one around for miles, Megan very slowly took off her bright blue Windbreaker, high-top sneakers, socks, and blue jeans. Then, wearing only her T-shirt and her underwear, Megan closed her eyes and gingerly stepped into the cold water.

After about an hour of swimming, sunning,

and splashing, the two teenage girls climbed back on the shore, put on their clothes, packed up their camera equipment, and headed home on their bicycles. Her wet underwear made Megan very uncomfortable as she rode her bike, so she pedaled as hard as she could, racing to get home quickly and change into some dry clothes.

Megan was so busy pedaling that she did not even notice when a mysterious unmarked gray truck carrying three large metal barrels drove up from another area of the lake, and headed off down an old dirt road.

It was already dark by the time Megan got home from her trip to the lake. She felt so tired she barely had the strength to stop in the kitchen to mutter a "hello" to her mother, Dee, and her ten-year-old brother, Will. Dee and Will were eating fried chicken and mashed potatoes at the table, while Lassie, the family purebred collie, was slurping away at her water bowl in the corner of the room. Dee motioned to Megan to join them for dinner. Although fried chicken and mashed potatoes were some of Megan's favorite foods, she was really tired, and she had a tremendous headache, so Megan turned down the offer and went straight upstairs to bed without eating any dinner at all.

About an hour later, Chris McCulloch, Megan and Will's father, came home from a business meeting with some of the members of the license and permit department of the Glen Ridge Town Council. He needed a special permit so his construction firm could begin work on a new housing project. As he opened the door, Chris could hear the steady beat of the music on Dee's aerobic workout tape. He stood in the doorway for a minute, watching Dee work out in the living room. It was a funny sight—his wife jumping, reaching, and stretching to the beat of the music, while his dog lay lazily on the floor, watching her.

Eventually, Dee pooped out, turned off the tape, and lay still on the floor, moving only to wipe the sweat from her brow. Chris bent over and gave her a big kiss hello.

Dee looked up at her husband and grinned. "Do I know you?" she teased.

"I'm the guy who thinks you're good-looking," he replied with a smile.

Lassie padded over to Dee and Chris and nosed her way between their faces. Then she stuck out her long wet tongue and licked Chris right on the nose.

"And Lassie's the girl who thinks you're good-looking," Dee said, laughing as Chris wiped the wet dog kiss from his face.

Dee jumped up. "You hungry?" she asked.

Chris rubbed his stomach. "Starving," he answered as he followed Dee into the kitchen. Then he noticed that the house was unusually quiet. At this time on most nights, Megan's stereo would be blasting, and Will and Lassie would be wrestling in front of the TV. But tonight, the kids were nowhere to be seen or heard.

"Where are the rest of the troops?" he asked.

"Will's doing homework," Dee said as she turned on the oven.

"You're kidding!" Chris joked, clutching his heart while pretending to be in shock. His son was not known for his terrific study habits.

Dee laughed. "Nope. He's over at Andy Glover's. I'm going to pick him up in a half hour. Megan skipped supper and went to bed early."

"Probably caught a bug or something," Chris said as he peered into the refrigerator. "Think I'll go check on her."

Dee watched as he headed out of the kitchen and up the stairs to Megan's bedroom, Lassie following close at his heels.

Chris knocked softly at Megan's door. When she didn't answer, he silently opened the door, and tiptoed over to her bed. The room was completely dark, except for a small nightlight in the corner of the room by her desk. The tiny glimmer of light cast an eerie shadow on the faces of the rock and roll stars that smiled down from the many posters on Megan's walls.

Megan was lying on her side, fast asleep, breathing ever so softly into her pillow. Chris bent down and felt Megan's forehead for fever. She felt a little warm. Probably just a slight temperature, he thought to himself. Taking care not to wake her, Chris straightened the covers around his daughter, and turned to leave the room.

Lassie looked down at the floor by Megan's bed. Lying there was Megan's old scarecrow doll, the one that had been her favorite when she was about five years old. She had named it Crow. As a kid, Megan had dragged Crow everywhere, and now the old doll was missing an eye, and had lost half its stuffing. But Megan still loved the doll. Even though she was now fourteen years old, and much too old for rag dolls, Megan insisted on keeping Crow in her room, despite the doll's mangled condition.

Lassie picked Crow up in her teeth and offered it to Chris. Chris smiled and took the old doll from the jaws of the kind, caring collie. With a loving smile, Chris tucked the doll between Megan's curved arms.

Taking one last look at his sleeping daughter, Chris turned and walked out of the room, leaving the door slightly ajar for Lassie to follow. But Lassie stayed behind, settling down on the floor beside Megan's bed. Lassie always liked to be around the members of her family whenever they were sick. She would lie by the sick person's bedside, quiet as a mouse, waiting for just the right time to give a comforting kiss, or to gently lay her long, noble head in the lap of the ailing family member.

So tonight Lassie made herself comfortable in Megan's room, stretching out on the floor and resting her head on her front paws. Then she looked up through her slanted collie eyes and prepared to keep watch over Megan for a while.

CHAPTER
2

The next day, Megan felt even sicker than she had the night before. Her bones were achey, her stomach felt queasy, and she was running a temperature.

"No school for you today," Dee said to her, clicking her tongue at the unusually high numbers that registered on the thermometer. "You just rest here in bed for a while." Dee tried to smile cheerfully at Megan, but she had a tough time masking her concern for her daughter. Megan's temperature was dangerously high. It did not make sense, Dee thought to herself. Just yesterday morning, Megan was fine. She had come home early, and run out to do some homework assignment with Lisa. A few hours later, Megan had come down with this odd sickness.

After making sure Megan was comfortable, and that she had enough orange juice on her night table, Dee shut Megan's bedroom door and ran downstairs to call the doctor.

Now ordinarily, a day at home with nothing to do but listen to the stereo and watch soap operas on TV would have made Megan very happy. But today she felt so awful that she decided it would be worth going back to school—if only she would feel better!

Megan spent most of the morning sleeping—waking only long enough to take a sip of orange juice to soothe her parched throat before falling back asleep.

While Megan slept, Dee worked downstairs at her desk in the family room. Dee ran her own personnel business which matched up business people with employees for their firms. Usually Dee was a very concentrated worker. But today, she just could not keep her mind on her work. The doctor had told her that Megan's illness did not sound like the flu, and that she should keep an eye on her, making sure that she didn't get any worse. Dee had been running up and down the stairs, checking on Megan every half hour or so, but each time the scene in the room had been exactly the same—Megan lying fast asleep on her bed, and Lassie lying on the floor next to her, watching. Lassie hadn't moved an inch from her post all night. It took a lot of convincing and stern orders from Dee to get the loyal, loving collie to go downstairs, eat some breakfast, and go outside for a little exercise.

SCREECH! A high-pitched whine coming from outside the house interrupted Dee's thoughts. She jumped up from her chair and went out onto the porch to see what the commotion was about. She smiled briefly as she saw Will turn the corner on his skateboard, carrying a brown paper bag in one hand. Lassie was charging along at top speed by his side, her bushy brown and white tail wagging happily behind her. It didn't take long for the fun-loving collie to dart past Will on the way to the house. Will pumped even harder with his free foot as he tried to catch up with the speeding collie, but his face registered a feeling of true frustration as he watched Lassie dart across the front lawn, making a beeline right for the front porch of the house.

Lassie lay down right at Dee's feet, her paws stretched out in front of her, her head resting on her long, lean legs. She watched Will as he screeched to a stop at the edge of the lawn, flipped his skateboard up with his foot, caught it in one hand, and followed Lassie onto the porch. Will couldn't be sure, but the way Lassie's long mouth was pulled back around her teeth, he felt as though the collie was laughing smugly at him.

"Okay, so you beat me again. But you cheated again, so now we're going to try to make it the best three out of four!" Will grunted to Lassie.

"RUFF!" Lassie barked in response, jumping up onto all fours. She had not cheated at all. It wasn't her fault that Will was not allowed to use his skateboard on the lawn.

"You guys sure make enough noise," Dee said with a smile as she put her arm around Will and took him inside for lunch, Lassie padding quietly behind them.

"It wasn't us. It was this old skateboard," Will argued.

Dee choked back a laugh. Will had been trying to convince her to buy him a new skateboard for months.

"I have one word for you," she said. "Oil."

Will grinned. "I have two words . . . no use."

"What's in the bag?" Dee changed the subject.

"Ice cream, for Megan. How is she?"

Dee frowned. "Worse than awful. Hey, you're melting," she said, pointing to the wet bag in Will's hand.

Will looked down to find Lassie happily licking up some delicious melted strawberry ice cream that had leaked on to the kitchen floor. When she had finished, Lassie looked up at Will with her mouth wide open—she wanted more!

"That's it for you." Will laughed, stroking Lassie on the top of her head. Then he went over to the kitchen cabinet, pulled down two bowls, and started to dish out some ice cream. Then he headed up to Megan's room, ice cream in hand. Lassie followed him up the stairs, moving right under the bowls—just in case she had a chance to lick up any more melted ice cream!

Megan's door was half open. Will peeked in and saw his sister lying slumped in her bed, dozing while she listened to her stereo through her headphones. Her face was almost as white as the sheets on her bed, and there were beads of sweat on her forehead.

Lassie used her long, pointed nose to push the door open, and walked over to her post by

the side of Megan's bed. Will followed close behind and sat right down on the edge of Megan's
bed.

The movement of the bed woke Megan.
Blinking her eyes for a second, she took off her
headphones and sat up a little taller. Then she
glanced at her clock. It was almost a quarter to
one in the afternoon.

"What are you doing here?" she asked her
brother.

"Came home for lunch. Hey, are you just
goofing off because you're late with homework?"

Megan got annoyed. "I don't 'goof off'," she
said irritably. "I'm really sick."

"Oh yeah?" Will said, unconvinced. "Then
I guess you won't want any ice cream." He
smiled as he ate a heaping spoonful of the thick,
pink dessert.

Just the thought of food made Megan's
stomach do flip-flops. She crossed her hands over
her belly and made a face. "Yech . . . "

Will looked concerned. If Megan didn't
want strawberry ice cream—her favorite—then
she really must be sick. He put her bowl of ice
cream on the floor for Lassie. The dog gave a
"woof" of thanks, and then proceeded to dig into
the ice cream with her long, fast-moving tongue.

"You're not catching, are you?" Will asked Megan with genuine concern.

"No . . . at least I don't think I am."

Will was not taking any chances. He got up from the bed and moved across the room to lean against the bureau.

"Will . . . what are you doing after school?" Megan asked slowly, with more than a drop of sweetness in her voice.

Will knew that tone of voice very well. His big sister used it whenever she wanted him to do her a favor. Well, he wasn't falling for it this time, no sirree!

"I'm busy," he said quickly.

Megan leaned toward Will, but she felt too dizzy to sit up that far. Exhausted, she leaned back against her pillows.

"Look, all I need is a few more pictures to finish my photography class homework. The burned chimney, a shaft of sunlight, a broken beam . . . "

"What are you talking about?" Will broke in. Megan never even let him breathe on her precious camera. Now she wanted him to use it to take pictures of some chimney? She must be delirious, he thought half jokingly to himself.

"Haven't you always wanted to use my camera?" Megan asked him. "Well, this is your chance."

"Your assignment must be pretty important," Will answered her. Then he put his bowl on the bureau, and walked over to the far corner of the room where Megan's most precious possession—her camera—was lying in its case on a chair. Will opened the bag and took out the beautiful, black, state-of-the-art 35-millimeter camera. He handled it delicately. He smiled mischievously as he turned the lens toward himself and looked through the viewfinder the wrong way—knowing just how much this would irk Megan. He laughed as she gave him a dirty look. Finally he walked over and handed her the camera.

As she showed Will how to load the film and work the different lenses, Megan felt a little guilty. She knew her parents would not approve of her asking Will to do her homework assignment. "Will . . . " she said, in a quiet whisper. "Don't tell Mom and Dad you helped me."

Will understood. "Okay," he promised.

All afternoon in school, Will watched the clock. When the bell finally rang at three-thirty, he raced home, picked up Megan's camera bag, hopped onto his bicycle, and headed for the wooded area that Megan had carefully mapped out for him. As he rode, Lassie galloped at his side, keeping pace with the fast-moving bicycle as it moved quickly down the old dirt road and across a rickety wooden bridge. When they finally reached the lake, Will hopped off his bike and looked around.

The trees by the lake were so dense they practically blocked out all the sunlight, making the forest dark and scary. Will motioned for Lassie to stay with him. He was glad not to have to be alone in such a creepy place.

"Stay close, Lassie," he whispered. Finally, Will and Lassie reached the pile of ashes that was the subject of Megan's photography project. It seemed so ominous that Will shuddered slightly.

"You think anybody ever lived here?" he asked Lassie nervously. Then he took out the list of photographs Megan wanted him to take. "Sunlight, burned chimney, broken beam . . . " Will laughed out loud. "She must have some teacher!"

"Ruff!" Lassie barked in agreement. Will petted her lovingly on the head. Then he pulled the camera out of its case, loaded the film just as Megan had shown him, and started to shoot pictures of the chimney. At first he was a bit shaky. But with each click of the camera shutter, Will grew more confident.

Lassie had nothing to do while Will was taking pictures, so the curious collie decided to do some exploring. She started by sniffing the ground and scratching at some rocks. She caught a glimpse of a brilliantly colored monarch butterfly out of the corner of her eye, and took off into the nearby brush to chase after it.

In no time at all, Will had finished taking the pictures on Megan's list. He was anxious to get home and tell his big sister what a terrific job he had done. He looked around for Lassie. "Lassie!" he called into the woods. "Lassie, come!"

After a moment or two, Lassie appeared at the edge of the brush. She hesitated for a moment, looking sadly at Will.

"Come on," Will urged her. "Let's get out of this place. It'll be dark soon."

But Lassie didn't go to Will. Instead, she turned and headed into the heavy underbrush, motioning with her head for Will to follow. Will watched her for a minute. Then he looked up into the trees. The sun was setting and the forest was even spookier than before. He didn't want to follow Lassie any deeper into the woods. He just wanted to go home. Still, he thought, it was better to go into the brush with Lassie, than to stand all alone by the burned-out house without her. So, reluctantly, Will ducked down and followed Lassie into the brush.

The prickly thorns of the plants scratched at Will's arms as he followed Lassie farther and farther into the brush. Finally, when she had just about reached the lake, Lassie stopped. Will stood back and watched as she sniffed at the ground with her nose, and whined softly. Finally the boy walked over to her and looked down at the ground.

"Ugh!" he cried. Will could feel his stomach turn as he looked down. There, at the bank of the lake was a pile of decaying dead fish, and the carcasses of two dead jackrabbits.

Will was feeling queasy. "Let's get out of here, now!" he shouted to Lassie. "Lassie! Come!"

Lassie had a feeling that the poor creatures at her feet had not died normal deaths. She wanted to stay and find out just what was causing these mysterious deaths. But Will was determined to get home as fast as he could.

"Lassie! Come!" he ordered again. Slowly, with her tail lying low behind her, Lassie moped out of the brush. She looked back once or twice before taking off and running close beside Will as he hopped on his bike and pedaled down the dirt road and back toward his home, moving as fast as his legs could carry him!

CHAPTER
3

"Dead!" Megan screeched weakly from her bed. "I don't want to hear about dead things!"

As soon as Will had reached the house he had parked his bike and hightailed up the stairs to his sister's room. The sight of the dead animals on the bank of the lake had made him nervous and upset. He was anxious to share the story with someone, just to make himself feel better.

Megan tried to prop herself up on the pillows while she talked to Will, but she was even weaker than she had been in the afternoon, so she stayed as she was, lying flat against sheets that were damp with perspiration. Her body alternated between being too cold and too hot, her head was pounding, and every muscle in her body seemed to be aching. Her eyes could not stand the glare of bright light, so the shades in her room were drawn, and only the study lamp on her desk was turned on. Will's vivid description of the decaying bodies of dead animals did not help the sick feeling in her stomach, either. Quickly, Megan struggled to change the subject.

"Did you take the pictures?" she asked.

Will sat up proudly, blew on his fingertips and rubbed them confidently on his chest. "Piece of cake. You should get an A at least."

"And my camera's still in one piece?"

"More or less," Will teased, as he took the camera bag off his shoulder and placed it carefully on the chair.

"Thanks, Will, really," Megan mumbled, trying to hold back an exhausted yawn. Then without another sound, Megan slumped down and drifted back to sleep.

Will turned off the study lamp, tiptoed out of the room, closed his sister's bedroom door, and walked quietly down the stairs for dinner.

Dinner was unusually quiet at the McCullochs's that night. On an ordinary evening, Megan and Will would be arguing about something or other, and Dee and Chris would be holding a conversation over the argument. But tonight, no one said a word throughout the whole meal. Everyone was far too busy worrying about Megan to carry on any type of normal conversation. Megan's temperature had leveled off, but it hadn't dropped. She had gotten a lot weaker since the morning, and she wasn't even able to hold down water. The doctor did not know what was wrong with her, so there was nothing the McCullochs could do but wait and see what happened. The waiting made dinner seem unusually tense. Dee and Chris occasionally looked up from their food to catch each other's worried glances, and Will ate his meal as quickly as he could, anxious to get out of the room before either of his parents had a chance to ask him what he had done that afternoon after school. Even Lassie seemed depressed— she barely touched her food.

Finally, Will asked to be excused. Instead of going into the living room for his evening romp with Lassie, Will went straight up to his room and closed the door. Lassie padded after him. But rather than following Will into his room, the collie nosed her way past Megan's half shut bedroom door, and went right back to her place beside the sick girl's bed.

Downstairs, Chris sat at his desk, trying to catch up on some of his paperwork, while Dee finished straightening things up in the kitchen. The uneasy quiet was interrupted by the high-pitched ringing of the living room phone. Dee raced over to take the call.

"Hello," she answered. Chris sat up and listened to his wife's conversation.

"Hi, Emily, how are you? Oh no . . . How bad is she . . . I see . . . No, I talked with the doctor again. He doesn't think Megan has a virus." Dee paused for a second while she listened to the voice on the other end. Chris knew Dee was thinking about something, because she was twisting a short lock of her hair around her finger. That was what his wife always did when she was in the middle of figuring out the solution to a problem. Finally she spoke again.

"Yes, Emily, of course. Let's keep in touch. Goodbye," Dee said as she hung up the phone.

"Who was that?"

"Emily Franklin . . . " Dee answered. Chris gave her a blank look. He didn't know any Emily Franklin.

"Lisa's mom," Dee explained. "She said Lisa's not feeling well, either. She has symptoms like Megan's. She wondered if Megan has told us anything."

"Why?" Chris asked. "What's Lisa told her?"

"Nothing. But maybe we should go talk to Megan," Dee said as she moved toward the stairs.

Dee knocked quietly on Megan's door. "Megan, honey, are you awake?" she asked softly.

"Come in," Megan murmured from under her covers.

Dee and Chris walked in quietly, and gingerly sat on the edge of Megan's bed.

Dee ran her fingers softly through Megan's long blonde hair. "Megan, honey," she began softly, "I just got off the phone with Lisa's mom. She said Lisa's feeling as awful as you are. And Dad and I were just wondering what you and Lisa were doing yesterday afternoon. I think that might give us a clue to what might have made you both feel so bad."

Megan looked from her mother to her father. Maybe they were right. Maybe she and Lisa *had* gotten sick while they were taking the pictures of the burned-out house by the lake. So, after taking a deep breath, Megan told her parents about the homework assignment, the burned-out house, and the lake. When she got to the part about swimming around in the water in just her T-shirt and underpants, she got very embarrassed. Her face turned bright red and she scrunched down under the covers. She looked away from her parents.

"It's okay, honey," Chris said gently as he tried to urge her to finish her story.

"Well, it was too late to finish my assignment," Megan continued, "so I asked Will to help. And when he went out there with Lassie, they found some dead animals."

Chris looked anxiously at Dee. "Dead . . . " he muttered under his breath. Then, noting the panic on Megan's face, he forced himself to smile at her soothingly as he smoothed the covers round her.

"I'll go out there first thing in the morning to see what's up," he said reassuringly. Then he and Dee stood, and started for the door.

"There could be something wrong with that water . . . " he whispered to Dee.

"I'm going to call the doctor," Dee told him as they walked downstairs.

*　　*　　*

The very next morning, just as he had promised, Chris drove out to the area around the burned-out house. Lassie went along for the ride. She sat in the front seat of the family's black 4×4, letting the wind blow at her face while she stuck her long, collie nose out of the half opened side window. Chris drove along the old dirt road, keeping his eyes peeled for any sight of the old house. When he finally saw the chimney and the ashes, he stopped the car and climbed out. Lassie moved across the seat and followed him. Chris looked around for a minute, searching for some sign of the dead animals. When he found none, he turned to his guide, Lassie.

"Show me," he said to the wise collie.

Lassie knew exactly where she was. Already her amazing sense of smell was picking up the pungent odor of rotting fish. She sniffed at the ground as she led Chris into the same brush she and Will had crawled through the day before. But before Lassie could reach the lake, she stopped short. She picked up her regal head and stood very quietly. Her hairy, triangular ears stood straight up on the sides of her head, twitching slightly. Lassie heard something moving far off in the bushes. Chris watched her carefully, sensing almost immediately that something was wrong. He knew that although *he* had not heard anything unusual, Lassie certainly had, and that within a matter of minutes, she would lead him to the trouble.

Once Lassie had figured out the direction the noise was coming from, she began to move slowly to the left, through a patch of thick, overgrown bushes. After a few feet she stopped and motioned over to the lake with her head.

Chris looked in the direction of her eyes. What he saw made him furious! There, parked by the edge of the water was the same unmarked gray truck Megan had unknowingly passed just two days before. Five metal barrels were stacked in the back of the truck. Two men were holding a sixth barrel over the water, and spilling a thick, slimy, foul-smelling, greenish-brown liquid into the clear lake water.

"Grrrr!" Lassie snarled, baring the sharp teeth of her bottom jaw. Chris was not the only one who was angered by the actions of the two men. With a quick start, Lassie darted out of the bushes toward the truck. Chris followed close behind her.

The two men heard Lassie's ominous growl and looked at each other in surprise. Within a

matter of seconds, the men jammed the barrel
into the back of the truck and tried to jump into
the front cab. The driver managed to get behind
the wheel safely. But before the other man could
climb into the passenger seat, Chris tapped him
on the shoulder.

"Got a minute?" he asked through angry,
clenched teeth.

The man turned around quicker than Chris
had expected and swung his left fist right at
Chris's nose. But Chris was just as fast, and he
delivered a good solid hit of his own, right to the
man's stomach.

The man bent over in pain and stared up at
Chris through glazed eyes. Chris was about to
pull back and throw another punch, when the
man stood suddenly, and raised his leg in a powerful kick. His foot landed squarely on Chris's
side, just missing his kidney. Chris grunted in
pain.

Without so much as a bark or a growl of
warning, Lassie leaped to Chris's aid, biting at
the legs of the attacker and jumping up to grab
him by the collar. But the dog was not fast
enough, and before she knew it, the man had
landed one more punch to Chris's side. Lassie

watched helplessly as Chris fell to the ground, clutching his stomach and his nose.

With a nasty snicker, Chris's opponent climbed into the cab of the truck next to his pal and slammed the door. The driver of the truck started the engine and crashed through the underbrush onto the old dirt road.

"RUFF! RUFF!" Lassie barked with all her might as she raced on her strong, muscular collie legs through the brush onto the dirt road after the truck. Collies are great runners and they can catch almost any four-legged animal in the forest, but they just aren't fast enough to catch up with a four-wheeled gasoline-powered truck. Before long, the truck had disappeared from Lassie's sight.

Lassie stood tall in the middle of the road and watched as the truck drove off, leaving a trail of flying dirt and gasoline exhaust behind it. As she stood with her great white chest panting for air, she heard an almost inaudible moan of pain from behind her. She turned back toward the lake, only to see Chris, her beloved master, lying motionless in a shallow part of the lake. The lower half of his body was covered with water, and his head was lying on top of a sharp rock that rose up above the water level.

A trickle of blood was dripping from his cheek, turning the lake water a rusty brown.

Lassie found a break in the thick, prickly underbrush, and dashed over to the steep bank of the lake. Quickly she jumped into the lake and, keeping her head above water, the dog used her front paws to paddle her way through the ice cold water over to Chris's still body.

As soon as Lassie reached Chris, she began to tug at his shirt collar with her strong teeth. If only she could get a good grip on Chris's shirt and tug him to safety at the low bank of the lake! Lassie clutched his shirt collar tightly between her powerful jaws, and pulled and pulled with all her might. But the mighty collie just wasn't strong enough to budge her master from his spot on the rock.

Lassie needed help if she was going to get Chris out of the polluted water. She looked around into the forest. There wasn't a soul to be seen for miles around. Lassie was afraid to leave Chris alone, but she knew that if he were left in the polluted water for too long he would surely die.

"RUFF! RUFF! RUFF!" Lassie barked frantically, hoping someone on the main road would hear her and come to Chris's aid.

CHAPTER
4

"Ruff! Ruff!" Lassie waited impatiently for someone to answer her call, but the area by the lake was deserted. In fact, the lack of visitors to the area was exactly what made the lake the perfect dumping ground for disposing of hazardous waste. The criminals were sure no one would come by and catch them in the act. They had not counted on Chris showing up and interrupting their illegal dumping.

Lassie whined with compassion as she looked down at Chris. He was lying motionless in the water, and his breathing was becoming more and more shallow and irregular. Lassie tried one more time to pull him up the bank to safety but the limpness of his body made him seem much heavier than he really was. Finally, the determined collie was forced to give up. She was never going to save Chris this way!

Lassie did not want to leave Chris alone, especially because she always felt it was her duty to be with a sick or injured member of her family. But she knew she had no other choice. She had to leave the area and run for help. So, with one last sorrowful look at Chris, Lassie swam back to the bank and climbed up onto the shore.

Lassie took only a second to shake the polluted water from her body. Then she ran off at top speed toward home—and help! The collie looked like a blazing shooting star as she raced over the rickety bridge, along the old dirt road, past the tall, green trees of the forest and across an open field. By the time she reached her own neighborhood, Lassie was tired and out of breath. But she knew she could not take a rest stop now. She just had to keep running! To save valuable time, Lassie took a short cut through the neighbors' lawns.

Springing off from her powerful collie legs, Lassie jumped over the neighbors' high wooden fences with so much ease it seemed she could fly. Lassie was in such a hurry that she barely noticed the pain she felt in her hind legs when she crashed back down to the ground.

Finally Lassie reached the street in front of the McCullochs's house. There was a crowd of ten-year-old boys playing basketball in a neighbor's driveway. Half the boys were wearing T-shirts, half were not wearing shirts at all. That was how they could tell who was on which team. Lassie stood for a minute, picking Will out of the crowd. She found him very quickly, he was one of the boys on the "shirts" team.

"Ruff! Ruff! Ruff!" she called frantically to Will. But Will was too busy playing basketball to notice her call. He ignored the barking and called to his teammate to pass the ball.

"Over here! Over here!" Will called from under the basket, waving his hands in the air.

Lassie knew this was no time for games. She was going to have to break it up. Moving purposefully, Lassie barged right into the middle of the game and stopped at Will's feet.

"Ruff! Ruff!"

Will stopped short and looked curiously at his beloved collie. "Lassie! What are you doing here?" he asked.

Everyone watched as Lassie answered him by running a few feet down the sidewalk. Then she stopped and faced Will.

"Ruff! Ruff!" Lassie barked. Then she moved a few more steps down the walk.

"Something's wrong!" Will explained quickly to his friends. "I gotta go!"

"Hey! You can't leave! We're playing three on three!" one of his teammates yelled angrily after him. But Will ignored the call. He figured that if Lassie had run to get him, she must *really* need his help. Breathlessly, Will hopped on his bike and pedaled off down the street, following Lassie.

It took a few minutes for Will to recognize the route they were taking, but eventually the trees, the old wooden bridge, and the dirt road began to look familiar. Lassie was bringing him back to the lake. Will shivered nervously. Between the dead fish, the rabbit carcasses, and the burned-out house, that whole area really gave Will the creeps! Still, Will figured that Lassie must have a good reason for dragging him back down to the lake, so he followed her without question.

Before long, Lassie had led Will back to the burned-out house Will had photographed as a favor to Megan. Will hopped off his bike and leaned it up against a tree. Lassie waited impatiently for him. Finally she barked a loud order for him to follow her down to the lake.

On the way to the lake, the boy and his dog passed by Chris's parked 4×4. Suddenly Will got very scared. Dad must be in real trouble, he thought anxiously. Will ran up to the 4×4 and peeked inside, hoping his father would be there. But when he looked in the open window, all he saw was an open map sprawled across the backseat, and a pair of sunglasses resting on the ledge above the dashboard. Will's heart began to pound furiously with fear. Where was his father? And what kind of trouble had he gotten himself into?

"RUFF!" Lassie's bark shocked Will back to reality. He jumped to attention and raced off into the brush after Lassie. Somehow Will knew instinctively that every second wasted could mean disaster for Chris.

"Dad! Dad!" Will called as he and Lassie made their way out of the brush and over to the lake. "Dad! Where are you?"

The sound of his son's voice reached Chris's semiconscious ears. He opened his eyes very slowly and tried to get his bearings. He was almost too weak to move, but Chris mustered up all the strength he had left to call back to his son.

"Will," he answered weakly.

Will followed Lassie's lead down to the bank of the lake. He felt a little faint at the sight of his father lying there in the lake water. But Will knew this was no time to panic. The boy pulled himself together and shouted down to his father.

"Dad! I'm coming down!" Will started down toward the lake, looking for a steady pathway along the slope. As he tried to get his footing, Will slid a few feet down the wet, slippery hill.

"Will!" Chris moaned. "Keep out of the water! You'd better go for help."

Will knew he could never leave his father alone now. "I want to stay with you," he said defiantly. Will could hear loud rustling behind him. He turned quickly, only to find Lassie pulling feverishly at a broken tree branch that was lying in the bushes nearby. Will rushed over to help the struggling collie. He grabbed onto the branch with two hands and pulled. Between the boy and the collie, they had just enough strength to pull the branch loose from the fallen tree.

Will grabbed the long branch and walked back over toward the lake. Holding his end with both hands, Will held the other end out for Chris to grab. Desperately, Chris reached for the outstretched branch. His fingers just brushed the wood, but the branch was too far away for him to reach it. Chris watched in fear as his son moved closer to the lake.

"Be careful!" he warned.

Lassie watched as Will struggled to help his father. She wanted to help, too. Barking loudly, the brave collie darted off toward the water.

"Lassie! No!" Will ordered her. Lassie looked at Will. She could see he meant business. Quietly, she moved out of the way.

Will dug his feet firmly into the steep, muddy bank. Then he bent down and reached as far as he could toward the water. Chris struggled to reach the dangling branch. Finally he grasped the very tip of it. It took more strength than Will ever knew he had to slowly pull his father out of the polluted water and up onto the bank. Chris tried to help, but the combination of the polluted water and the injuries he had gotten while fighting left Chris with little strength to help. Still, father and son worked together as a team, and after awhile, Chris found himself lying safely in the mud about halfway up the bank of the lake. Will moved carefully down the slope to reach his father. As soon as he got close enough, Will reached out and grabbed his father in a big bear hug. Chris returned the hug, holding on to Will as tightly as he could.

It wasn't until Chris was strong enough to walk back up the slope that they noticed that Lassie had been very quiet. When they reached the field at the top of the slope, they found out why.

Lassie was lying still on her side along the edge of the dirt road. Her eyes were shut, and her beautiful white chest was barely moving up and down with each difficult, irregular breath she took. Lassie was very sick. It had taken her last bit of strength to fetch Will and bring him to Chris's aid. Now the brave, unselfish collie had no strength left at all. She lay helpless, unable to move.

CHAPTER
5

Dee glanced nervously at the clock in the kitchen. It read ten past five. Dee sighed uncomfortably. It had been almost three hours since Chris had called her from the doctor's office and told her the story about the lake, the fight, and Lassie's heroism. Chris had told her that he and Will were going to the family doctor's office first, and then they were rushing Lassie to the veterinarian. Neither doctor was very far from the house, and it certainly seemed to Dee that it was taking an awfully long time for them to get home.

Dee paced back and forth across the kitchen floor. Megan was in the kitchen, too. She was finally starting to feel better, so she had come downstairs for a bowl of her mother's home-made chicken vegetable soup. Megan watched as her mother paced back and forth with a worried look on her face. Seeing her mother so frantic made Megan nervous, too. She tried to interest Dee in a conversation, just to distract her.

"The soup is great, Mom," Megan complimented her. Dee glanced over to Megan and muttered a polite thanks.

Dee and Megan both jumped a bit as they heard the motor of the 4×4 pull up in the driveway.

"They're here!" Megan announced as she leaped up from her seat at the kitchen table.

Dee smiled broadly as she saw Will walk through the kitchen door. But her smile disappeared abruptly as she saw her bandaged husband come up behind him. Chris was carrying Lassie in his arms. The brave purebred lay still in his arms with her brown eyes barely open. The scent of the familiar kitchen, and the sounds of the voices of her family drifted over toward Lassie, and she tried to lift her head and wag her tail to say hello. But hard as she tried, the collie's noble head would not budge, and her usually active tail stayed still.

"What did the doctor say?" Dee asked anxiously, glancing from Chris to Lassie.

"I'm okay . . . but the vet isn't sure about Lassie," Chris answered solemnly.

Dee looked at Will's sad expression. She walked over and gently placed a loving hand on his shoulder for support.

"She'll be all right."

Will looked up at her and choked back the tears that were starting to well up in his big blue eyes.

"It all depends how much water she swallowed from the lake," Will explained, quoting the veterinarian.

Will's head hung below his shoulders as he slumped out of the kitchen and up the stairs to his room. Chris followed him up the stairs, carrying Lassie as carefully as he could.

Megan watched them go and started to cry. She felt that Lassie's illness was all her fault. If only she hadn't listened to Lisa and gone swimming, none of this would have happened! Dee went over to Megan and held her close.

Will sat on his floor and leaned against his bed. Chris lay Lassie down on the floor and covered her with the extra blanket from Will's bed.

Chris stood there for a minute, watching as Will cradled the dog's head in his lap, and gently stroked the golden brown fur that covered her long neck. Chris tried to smile assuringly at his son as he closed the door and went back downstairs to his wife.

Will sat beside Lassie all night long, keeping watch over her with the same unfaltering concern with which the loyal collie kept watch over the human members of the McCulloch family when they were sick. It was just past midnight when Megan tapped lightly on Will's door and walked into the room.

"I couldn't sleep either," Megan said slowly. "Can I come in?"

Will would not even look up. Somehow he felt this whole mess was Megan's fault.

"Sure," he muttered.

Megan sat by Will's side and looked down at the sleeping collie.

"How is she?" Megan asked.

"I don't know," Will grumbled, refusing to look his sister in the eye.

The two sat quietly for a few seconds. Finally Megan brightened a little. "Will, Dad just has a little headache. And I feel lots better tonight . . . " she began.

"Lassie isn't better," Will interrupted gruffly.

Megan stood up and stared through guilty eyes at the ground. "I guess you think it's all my fault," she said slowly to Will. She waited for Will to disagree with her, to tell her that Lassie's illness wasn't any fault of her own. But Will didn't say a word. He sat absolutely still, staring at Lassie's motionless body.

"I guess it is all my fault," Megan sighed as she walked out of the room and gently closed the door.

Will heard Megan close her bedroom door. In the quiet of the night, Will heard the sounds of his sister's sobs as she cried herself to sleep.

Lying in the dark in their room, Chris and Dee heard Megan crying, too. But they felt it was better to let her cry it out and be by herself for a while than to run to her room and try to calm her down. Quietly, they continued their conversation.

"The police ran a check on the license plate on that truck," Chris told Dee. "They said it isn't the first time they've heard about dumping. It's just that no one's been willing to press charges."

Dee sat up and switched on the light on her

night table. "Why not?" she asked incredulously.

"Because NorthCo Chemical employs three thousand people," Chris explained.

Dee could feel her temper rising. "I can't believe no one's doing anything because they are afraid. Well I don't mind being a whistle-blower!" she exclaimed.

Chris bent over and kissed his wife on the lips. "I've always said you had a great pucker," he teased her.

As the sun rose early the next morning, the McCulloch house was still. Even Will had finally fallen asleep—sitting on the floor with his head propped up against his bed frame and his arms curved tightly around his beloved collie. All night the boy had tried his hardest to stay awake and keep his watchful eye on Lassie, but he had been so exhausted from the day's events that eventually sleep had taken over.

The light was just starting to stream in through Will's window when Lassie opened her eyes. She opened and closed them for a second in an attempt to blink out the sleep. Then she lifted her mighty head up to meet Will's. Playfully, Lassie used her pointy black nose to nuzzle the boy's face lovingly. Then she licked his face with her long, soft tongue.

It took awhile for Will to realize what had happened. But when he opened his eyes, the boy stared right into the bright, healthy eyes of his best friend—Lassie!

"Lassie!" he shouted as he hugged his collie across her broad back.

Lassie jumped up and kissed Will with such strength that she knocked him to the ground! Will giggled with delight as Lassie licked his face over and over with her thick pink tongue.

Lassie played with the enthusiasm of a puppy. She rolled over on her back and barked joyously as Will rubbed her soft white belly. Then she flipped over and jumped up onto Will's bed, her brown and white tail waving fast and furiously behind her. All the bad effects of the polluted water had left the collie's body, and she wanted to show Will how happy she was to feel better again.

Dee, Chris, and Megan were all awakened by Lassie's barks and Will's shouts of delight. They stood by the doorway to Will's room and smiled with relief at the sight of the boy and the dog playing.

"And I thought only cats had nine lives," Chris said out loud, looking at Lassie.

Will shrugged. He didn't care about how many lives cats had. He was just glad that his beloved Lassie had been given a second chance to live hers!

OTHER BOOKS FROM FANTAIL

FANTAIL

Young Indiana Jones and the Plantation Treasure by Rob McCay   014090218X

Young Indy Jones takes on more than he bargained for when he decides to help a beautiful young woman find a cache of treasure hidden by her late grandfather. The old man had been a plantation owner in South Carolina before the American Civil War. With the help of his journal, Indy and Lizzie set out to trace a former slave from the plantation, in whose hands lies the secret of the hidden treasure. But the intrepid boy is soon to discover that they are not the only ones on the trail . . .

Publishing date: May 1990

Young Indiana Jones and the Secret City by Les Martin   0140902163

Having witnessed the bizarre activities of an ancient sect posing as Whirling Dervishes, young Indy Jones finds himself in deadly danger during a trip to Turkey. Indy and his friend, Herman, are forced to fight for their lives in the vast maze of rooms and tunnels of a secret underground city. the rulars of this dark realm need only the blood of an innocent child to complete their evil rituals . . .

Publishing date: August 1990

Young Indiana Jones and the Circle of Death by Rob McCay   0140902171

A visit to an ancient British monument sparks off an
unexpected adventure for Indy and his friend, Herman. A
series of mysterious accidents have befallen a group
excavating
the lonely site of Stonehenge. Rumours of black magic and
supernatural incidents on Salisbury Plain lead Indy to
investigate the history of the standing stones but as the
darkest day of the year approaches, the Winter Solstice, the
boys find their lives threatened by the Dark Druids, an evil
sect with an unhealthy interest in human sacrifice!
Publishing Date: October 1990

Young Indiana Jones and the Tomb of Terror by Les Martin   0140902155

On holiday in Egypt, young Indiana finds himself in the
possession of a priceless gold ring and a mystery he is
determined to solve. His quest is to lead him far beneath the
Valley of the Kings to the hidden tomb of a boy Pharoah.
Braving the deadly snakes of an underground labyrinth and
the crocodile-infested waters of the Nile, Indy risks his life in
a dangerous bid to protect the tomb of Tutankhamon - there
are those whose hunger for gold will lead them to defy even a
Pharoah's Curse . . .
Publishing date: December 1990

Built to Last - 25 Years of the Grateful Dead by Jamie Jensen
0140902198

Not may rock groups have the insperation or the stamina to stick it out for 25 years, but then the Grateful Dead have never been just another rock 'n roll band. Ever since they burst onto the music scene in the psychedelic 1960s, the Grateful Dead have been doing things their own way and their unconventional approach to making music has earned them the unquestioning devotion of legions of fans around the world. Focusing on the unique experience of the Dead live in concert, with scores of photographs never seen before and interviews conducted on the eve of the first concert of the tour, this incredible book will put you in front-row centre at some of the best of the 2000-odd shows the Grateful Dead have played.